ONE WAY

ADOPT A DOG TODAY!

I LO♥E Dogs!

By Sue Stainton and Bob Staake

SCHOLASTIC INC.

ISBN 978-1-338-03113-3

Text copyright © 2014 by Sue Stainton. Illustrations copyright © 2014 by Bob Staake. All rights reserved. Published by Scholastic Inc., 557 Broadway, New York, NY 10012, by arrangement with Katherine Tegen Books, an imprint of HarperCollins Children's Books, a division of HarperCollins Publishers. SCHOLASTIC and associated logos are trademarks and/or registered trademarks of Scholastic Inc.

12 11 10 9 8 7 6 5 4 3 2   16 17 18 19 20 21

Printed in the U.S.A.

First Scholastic printing, February 2016

The artist used Adobe Photoshop 3.0 to create the digital illustrations for this book.
Typography by Jeanne L. Hogle

40

To Mum and Dad
—S.S.

To every cat that secretly wished
they'd been born a dog
—B.S.

ADOPT
A DOG
TODAY!

Dogs,
dogs,
dogs.

I love dogs!

Strong dogs,

long dogs.

Nosy dogs,

cozy dogs.

ADOPT
A DOG
TODAY!
→

Lazy dogs,

crazy dogs.

Chasing dogs,

racing dogs.

Speedy dogs,

greedy dogs.

Dogs in the snow,

dogs that know.

Dogs, dogs, dogs.

I love dogs!

Spotty dogs,

dotty dogs.

Wrinkly dogs,

crinkly dogs.

ADOPT
A DOG
TODAY!
→

Yappy dogs,

happy dogs.

ADOPT A DOG TODAY! →

Fluffy dogs,

scruffy dogs.

Prowling dogs,

howling dogs.

ADOPT A DOG TODAY!

Dogs in the park, dogs that bark.

Dogs, dogs, dogs.
I love dogs!

Curly dogs,

burly dogs.

Hairy dogs,

scary dogs.

Shaggy dogs,

waggy dogs.

Trendy dogs,

bendy dogs.

Sniffy dogs,

whiffy dogs.

Dogs that are famous,
dogs that are smart.
Dogs in the news,
dogs in fine art.

Dogs that wag tails,
dogs that chew bones.
Dogs in big houses,
dogs without homes.

Dogs, dogs, dogs.
I love dogs!